Danci

IN THE WINGS

Antonia Barber was born in London and grew up in Sussex. While studying English at London University, she spent her evenings at the Royal Opera House, where her father worked, watching the ballet and meeting many famous dancers. She married a fellow student and lived in New York before settling back in England. She has three children, including a daughter who did ballet from the age of three and attended the Royal Ballet School Junior Classes at Sadler's Wells.

Her best-known books are *The Ghosts*, which was runner-up for the Carnegie Medal and was filmed as *The Amazing Mr Blunden*, and *The Mousehole Cat*.

Antonia lives in an old oast house in Kent and a little fisherman's cottage in Cornwall.

If you like dancing and making friends, you'll love

DANCING SHOES

Lucy Lambert – Lou to her friends – dreams of one day becoming a great ballerina. Find out if Lucy's dream comes true in:

DANCING SHOES: LESSONS FOR LUCY
DANCING SHOES: INTO THE SPOTLIGHT
DANCING SHOES: FRIENDS AND RIVALS
DANCING SHOES: OUT OF STEP
DANCING SHOES: MAKING THE GRADE
DANCING SHOES: LUCY'S NEXT STEP
DANCING SHOES: BEST FOOT FORWARD
DANCING SHOES: TIME TO DANCE
DANCING SHOES: IN A SPIN
DANCING SHOES: MODEL DANCERS

And look out for more DANCING SHOES titles coming soon

Antonia Barber

DANCING SHOES
In the Wings

Illustrated by Biz Hull

PUFFIN BOOKS

PUFFIN BOOKS

Published by the Penguin Group
Penguin Books Ltd, 27 Wrights Lane, London W8 5TZ, England
Penguin Putnam Inc., 375 Hudson Street, New York, New York 10014, USA
Penguin Books Australia Ltd, Ringwood, Victoria, Australia
Penguin Books Canada Ltd, 10 Alcorn Avenue, Toronto, Ontario, Canada M4V 3B2
Penguin Books (NZ) Ltd, Private Bag 102902, NSMC, Auckland, New Zealand

On the World Wide Web at www.penguin.com

Penguin Books Ltd, Registered Offices: Harmondsworth, Middlesex, England

First published 2000
1 3 5 7 9 10 8 6 4 2

Text copyright © Antonia Barber, 2000
Illustrations copyright © Biz Hull, 2000
All rights reserved

The moral right of the author and illustrator has been asserted

Typeset in 15/22 Monotype Calisto

Made and printed in England by Clays Ltd, St Ives plc

British Library Cataloguing in Publication Data
A CIP catalogue record for this book is available from the British Library

ISBN 0–141–30845–1

Chapter One

Lucy Lambert heard the rattle of the letter box as she came out of the bathroom.

'I'll get the mail,' she called to her mother, and hurried upstairs in bare feet and a bathrobe.

The basement flat did have its own small letter box, but ever since the post woman had slipped on the wet steps one day, she preferred to put all the letters through the big brass flap in the main front door.

Emma was already trying to sort them out.

'It's mostly junk mail,' she told Lou, 'and some of those we've got three times over – one for us, one for you and one for Mrs Dillon!'

Emma's parents, Val and Peter Browne,

owned the big terraced house and they lived on the middle two floors. Lou, her mother, Jenny, and her little brother, Charlie, lived in the basement. It was a bit small for them but Lou didn't mind, because she liked sharing a house with Emma, who was her best friend. And then there was Mrs Dillon, who lived on the top floor. The old lady had once been a ballet dancer with the Russian Bolshoi Company. She had given Lou her first ballet lessons and both girls were very fond of her.

Emma handed Lou a bundle of letters and said, 'I think those are all yours. I'll take Mrs Dillon's for her.' She set off up the stairs.

'I'd better get dressed,' Lou called after her, 'if we're meeting Jem in the market.'

Sifting through the junk mail as she

went down, she found a letter with a Cornish postmark in her grandmother's neat handwriting. Another one, with a Canadian stamp, could only be from Auntie Helen. Then, underneath, she found a postcard of an angelic-looking Victorian child cradling a kitten. Someone had drawn bright-red spots all over the beautiful face and, turning the card over, Lou found that it was addressed to her and Emma. It read: 'URGH! I've got CHICKENPOX! HELP! HELP! I'm dying of boredom!' There was no name, only a little drawing of a shell at the bottom.

Lou dumped the pile of mail beside her mother's plate and told her, 'Shell's got chickenpox!'

'Poor thing,' said Jenny. 'She won't like that a bit.'

The others were already well into their breakfast, so Lou sat down and reached for the cereal packet.

'Is it serious?' she asked as she poured the milk.

'Chickenpox?' said her mother. 'No, not really, but it's an awful nuisance. You get itchy red spots and have to stay home from school in case you give it to anyone else.'

'She won't be able to do her modelling then,' said Lou, 'not if she's all spotty. I mean, are they big spots? Do you get a lot of them?'

But her mother had opened the letter from Auntie Helen and didn't seem to be listening. As she read it her face broke into a smile.

'Oh, Lou,' she said. 'You're going to have a cousin at last!'

Auntie Helen had been married about five years and Lou had almost given up hope. Everyone else at school seemed to have cousins.

'A baby?' she said. 'Oh, brilliant! Only I wish they didn't live so far away.'

Her mother had moved on to the other letter, so she asked, 'What does Grandma say?'

'Mmmm?' Her mother looked up. 'Well, she must have written this before she heard the news,' she said. 'It's about something quite different. She says one of her farmer friends in Cornwall has a big old barn that he is turning into cottages for visitors. Grandma thought Emma's dad might like to fit out the kitchens.'

'Oh, great!' Lou shovelled in the last of her cereal and said, 'Can I go up and tell him?'

Lou really liked Mr Browne, who had given up his job in a bank to become a carpenter.

'Better get dressed first,' said her mother.

Lou and Emma met Jem in the street market an hour later. Jem was Lou's other best friend and he was the only boy in their class at the Maple School of Ballet. Both girls were bursting with the news about Shell's chickenpox. They had met Shell Pink at a Summer Dance School the year before. She led a very glamorous life and did lots of modelling for children's clothes. But when Lou produced the postcard, Jem matched it with one of his own. Shell had sent him the Mona Lisa, covered in red spots, with the same cries of despair and boredom on the back.

'It must be really awful for her,' said
Emma.

'Oh, Shell likes to be different,' said
Jem heartlessly. 'Remember the blue hair
she had for that modelling job? I bet she
looks really stylish with red spots all
over!'

'You won't make jokes if you've caught

8

it,' said Emma reproachfully. 'It itches like mad!'

Jem shrugged. 'We can't have caught it. She didn't have it when we stayed over last weekend.'

'You can't always tell,' said Emma. 'I caught it from a cousin who was visiting us and he didn't get spots until he was back home.'

'Have you had chickenpox then?' asked Lou.

'Yes,' said Emma, 'when I was five. And you can't get it twice,' she added, sounding rather pleased with herself.

Lou frowned. 'How long is it before you know?'

'Oh, ages!' said Emma. 'I mean like *weeks*.'

'That's just *great*.' Lou turned to Jem. 'You know what this means ...'

Jem stared at her for a moment and then clapped his hand to his head. 'Oh, no!' he said.

'What? What is it?' Emma looked anxious now.

'Only that if we *do* get chickenpox,' said Lou, 'we might miss our Junior Associates ballet auditions!'

Chapter Two

There was less than a week to go before their auditions. The Junior Associates classes were run by the Royal Ballet School to help promising young dancers. Lou was thrilled when her ballet teacher arranged auditions for her and Jem. She desperately wanted them to win places. Now she began to have nightmares in which she appeared at the audition covered from head to toe in horrible red blotches.

Each morning she rang Jem, who would come to the phone moaning and protesting.

'Stop getting me up at the crack of dawn, Lou.'

'Have you got any?'

'Any what?'

'Have you got spots?' she would yell into her end of the phone.

'Er ... nope ... Don't see any. Now can I go back to bed?'

Then Lou would hang up the phone with a sigh of relief and the panic would die down a little until the next day.

Why couldn't I have had chickenpox when I was five, like Emma? she thought. It seemed so unfair that Emma was the one who couldn't catch it ... and she wasn't even *doing* the audition.

As the big day came closer, Lou grew

more and more anxious. It made her cross
and irritable. When her mother suggested,
quite reasonably, that her room needed
tidying, Lou flew into a temper.

'It's not my fault if there's things
everywhere!' she shouted. 'It's such a
poky little room. If I had a big room like

Emma's, with lots of cupboards and shelves and things, I could keep it tidy, instead of having to put everything in boxes!'

Her mother gave her a look, because of the shouting, but admitted that she did have a point. 'We really do need a larger flat,' she said thoughtfully.

At once Lou regretted the outburst. The last thing she wanted was to move away from Emma.

'Oh, it's all right, Mum,' she said quickly. 'I don't *really* mind. Look, I'm sorry I yelled at you …'

Her mother put an arm around her. 'I know you don't want to move,' she said, 'but with Charlie getting bigger, we do need more space.'

'We'll manage,' said Lou. 'Look, I'll go and tidy my room now.'

She hurried off and began stuffing
things out of sight under the bed.

When Emma came down a bit later,
Lou told her what had happened. Emma's
face fell.

'You don't really think your mum
would move, do you?'

'I don't know,' said Lou. 'I mean, now
she's got this job, we could afford a bigger
flat ... and she says Charlie is growing up.'

It was just one more anxiety to add to
the chickenpox. Lou grew fretful with
worry and tired from lack of sleep.

On the morning of the auditions she
woke up with a headache. Her mother
took her temperature and looked her over
carefully for any sign of spots.

'You're OK,' she said. 'It's probably just
nerves ...'

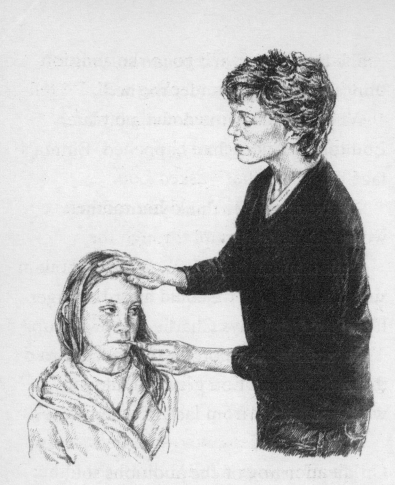

Lou moaned a bit. 'I don't feel well and I won't be able to dance properly and I just know I'm going to fail the audition.'

Jenny tried to comfort her. 'Look,' she said. 'I'll give you something for the headache. Then we'll go to the audition and if you're still not feeling well, I'll tell them and ask if we can change your audition to another day.'

'Can we do that?' asked Lou.

'I'm sure we can,' said her mother. 'They do auditions all through the summer term. Now, swallow this and then go back to bed for half an hour.'

When Lou woke again, the headache had gone ... only now her head felt as if someone had stuffed it with cotton wool.

She phoned Jem, who said he was fine.

'It's all in your mind, Lou,' he told her cheerfully. 'Remember what you were like when you did your first grade exam?'

Lou hadn't forgotten. She had been like a scared rabbit and it had taken a lot of effort on Jem's part to get her courage up.

'I suppose so,' she said.

'We'll pick you up in about twenty minutes,' he told her, and hung up.

Jem's grandad was driving them to the Royal Ballet Senior School, where the auditions were held. Lou was glad that she didn't have to face the Underground trains. Whether it was all in her mind or not, she was feeling distinctly fragile.

Chapter Three

Lou had seen pictures of the Royal Ballet
Junior School at White Lodge, a graceful
stone building in peaceful green parkland.
She had always imagined that the Senior
School would be a sort of bigger version
of the same thing. So it came as a nasty
shock to find that it was right in the city,
with a seriously noisy motorway on its
doorstep. This made parking very difficult
and by the time they had walked back to
the school door, the roar and fumes of the

traffic had started up her headache again.

But inside the building the noise faded to a distant hum and she tried to relax a little. Lots of other girls were arriving and a few boys. Some of the girls looked as scared as Lou, while others tossed their hair and talked to their mothers in loud, confident voices. One of those was Angela, a tall blonde girl who also went to the Maple School.

She said 'Hi!' to Jem, but ignored Lou because they weren't friends.

A slim, elegant lady who looked as if she might be a dancer came to welcome them. She told them that she was the auditions teacher and that she would be looking after them. She checked their names against a list and, after speaking a few friendly words to each one, gave them

a large number and some safety pins.
Then she led them away to the changing
rooms.

At this point Lou found to her dismay
that Jem and the other boys were going a
different way. Before she could say
goodbye or wish him good luck, he was
out of sight.

Her mother said, 'How are you feeling?'

Lou looked up at her and sighed. 'I'm OK,' she said.

'Are you sure that you want to go on with it?' asked Jenny. 'Because it's not too late to pull out.'

Lou was tempted. But then she would have to go through it all again, she thought, and without Jem.

'I'll be fine,' she said, and began pulling off her sweatshirt. Once she had got her ballet gear on, she told herself, she would feel quite different.

When they were all ready, with hair neatly groomed and the big black numbers pinned to the front of their leotards, the auditions teacher gathered them together. She explained that they would be going into a big studio where three assessors would be sitting at a table. There they would be put through a class of dance steps to see what they could do.

'Some of you look a bit nervous,' she said kindly, 'but it will be quite simple. Do your best and try to enjoy yourselves.'

They said goodbye to their mothers, some like Lou with a hug and a kiss, and others like Angela with a casual wave of the hand.

'Break a leg!' whispered Jenny, and Lou flashed her a smile, pleased that her mother had remembered how theatre people wished each other good luck.

'Now, I want you to form a line,' said the auditions teacher, 'and when we reach the studio I want you all to go in skipping and smiling!'

They formed a line and somehow Lou

ended up at the back. She trailed along the corridor behind the others and waited as they skipped away into the studio one by one. As the girl in front of her moved off, Lou tried hard to smile ... but the

smile only seemed to get as far as her mouth. Her eyes felt tired and heavy, and her feet seemed to be wearing boots as she skipped through the doorway.

Going home in the car, Lou had nothing to say. She sat in the back seat, between her mother and Jem's gran, with her eyes closed, listening to Jem in the front excitedly telling his grandad all about it. She felt sick and the headache was worse than ever. A feeling of misery came over her when she thought about the audition. She was sure that she had been really hopeless and that she was going to fail. When the results came, Jem would be accepted and so would Angela, and she would be left out ... I shall just crawl away into a corner and *die*, she thought ...

She was trying hard not to cry. Her left arm was itching and she pushed up her sleeve to scratch it. And it was then that she saw the first red spots.

Chapter Four

When Lou woke next morning, she itched
all over. It was almost a relief to know that
she really was ill. If she got sick with nerves
just because she had to perform in front of
strangers, her career as a ballet dancer
would be a short and unpleasant one! She
tried to remember what had happened the
day before, but the memory of the audition
was too painful and everything after that
seemed to be a blank. I must have fallen
asleep in the car, she thought.

She needed to go to the loo, so she
climbed out of bed and went through to
the bathroom. The sound of flushing
woke her mother, who was waiting for her
when she came out.

'How are you feeling?'

'Horrible!' said Lou. 'Headachy and
itchy.'

'Poor love! Well, try not to scratch.'

'I can't help it,' Lou protested. 'It's driving me mad!'

'It's hard, I know, but if you scratch, the spots may get infected and then they can leave little scars. If you don't scratch, they'll disappear as if they had never been.'

Lou sighed and decided not to scratch … but it wasn't easy. Jenny dabbed some calamine lotion on the itchiest spots, which helped a bit, but it made her look worse than ever. Now she had red spots *and* big white blotches!

Emma came down in her dressing gown to see how she was.

'I'm *hideous*!' said Lou, climbing back into bed, 'and I feel *awful*.'

She remembered the scars and peered closely at Emma. 'Do the spots really go away without leaving any marks?' she asked. It was hard to believe that she would ever look human again.

'Well, mine did,' said Emma comfortingly. 'I was only little and my mum made me wear white cotton gloves so that I couldn't scratch.'

'I wonder if Jem's got it?' said Lou, hoping that he had. It would be easier to bear if she had someone to share her misery.

Emma offered to phone him and returned a few minutes later to report. 'He says not a spot in sight and can he come round with his camera?'

'No, he can't!' said Lou crossly. 'No one except you and my mum is going to see me until all my spots have gone.'

Talking was making her feel worse, so she put her head under the duvet and went back to sleep.

When she woke up at lunch-time, she
didn't feel like eating so her mother
brought her a mug of chicken soup.

Emma came down again with the news
that Shell had phoned. 'I told her that
you'd got it and she said so have most

of the girls at her school. And she laughed … you know how she does.'

Lou did know. Shell Pink had a laugh that could shatter glass.

'But the good news is that she's getting better,' Emma went on. 'She hasn't got any new spots today and the ones she has got are starting to fade.'

They tried to work out when Shell had sent the postcards. It seemed likely that Lou would be spotty and off school for at least a week.

'Oh, I wish you hadn't already had chickenpox, Em,' said Lou. 'Then we could have had it together.'

'Actually,' said Emma, 'I think I'd rather *not*.'

'Well, no,' said Lou, 'but if you had, we could both have stayed home and done things together. Now I'll be all on my own.'

Emma was sympathetic ... but not *that* sympathetic.

The next day was very dull. The headache was a bit better but the spots were still coming. They had little blisters in the centre which dried up (if you didn't scratch them) and went scabby. What with the red spots and the yellow blisters and the brown scabs, not to mention the white blobs of calamine, Lou felt like crying every time she caught sight of herself in a mirror. But then she remembered that Shell had been through the same misery and was still laughing. If Shell can do it, so can I, she thought. Then, as if to reward her, Jenny put her head round the bedroom door and said, 'I thought you'd like to know, Jem's gran phoned and he's got it too.'

'Oh, *yes!*' said Lou, grinning for the first time in days. Now at least Jem wouldn't be able to tease her if she was still spotty when she went back to school.

Chapter Five

'How many spots have you got?' Lou was sitting by the phone in the hall with her duvet wrapped around her.

'Last time I counted it was six,' said Jem's voice cheerfully. He didn't sound as if he had a headache or anything.

'You'll have *loads* by tomorrow,' Lou told him heartlessly, 'and you'll feel *awful.*'

'I might not. My gran says some people get lots of spots and some get hardly any.'

'That's not fair!' Lou protested.

Jem just laughed.

It was a real comfort to have someone to talk to while Emma was at school. They chatted for quite a while, but then her mum said she needed the phone line so that she could use the Internet.

Jenny Lambert worked for a music professor at the local university. He was writing a book about a woman composer who had died young and Lou's mum helped with the research. The job was very important to her because it fitted in with looking after Charlie and Lou. The money she earned made a great difference to them all, so Lou gave up the phone without making too much fuss.

'I got you a couple of audio tapes from the library,' said Jenny. 'Why don't you go back to bed for a while and listen to one?'

There was a tape of a new book by
Lou's favourite author, so this seemed like
a good idea. It was better than daytime
television, which was all cookery and chat
shows and things for little children.

The book tape was good and Lou lay
with eyes closed for the next hour
listening to the story with the two cats,
Tina and Sassy, purring on her bed. Then
she needed a drink. She switched off the

tape and at once became aware of voices talking and the sound of laughter. Opening the door of her room, she listened again. One of the voices was her mother's and the other was a man's. They were talking the way people do when they know each other well.

Lou frowned. There weren't any men in her mother's life ... Well, not any who were close friends. Since Lou's father had died three years before, her mother had seemed content with only her children and her friends and neighbours for company. Lou had been pleased about this. She didn't like the thought of sharing her mum with someone else ... not someone who would take up a lot of her time and attention.

So who was this man, she thought crossly, and why hadn't her mother told her about him? Perhaps she wouldn't have found out about him at all if she hadn't had chickenpox … or not until it was *too late*. She remembered their friend Paul and how his life had gone all pear-shaped when his mother met a new man and married him instead of Paul's dad. 'Just hope *your* mum never marries again,' he had warned her.

Lou tiptoed quietly towards the door of the living room. It wasn't as if she was *spying* on her mum, she told herself, it was just because she didn't want the strange man to see her with the spots and the scabs and the blotches. But really she wanted to see how they behaved when they didn't know she was watching …

The door was half-open and luckily her mother had her back to it. The man was also half turned away and Lou thought he wouldn't notice her in the dark passageway unless he happened to look up. They were both holding mugs and Lou could smell the coffee. Their eyes were on the computer screen and Lou's mum was doing something with the mouse. They laughed again and talked

about something Lou didn't understand as they waited for the computer to download.

Looking at the man, Lou realized that she *had* seen him before. It was the man who had been talking to her mum in the street market, the day she and Paul had gone to Sammy's. And somewhere else – she searched her memory – at Jem's gran's party … the man had been there too, standing in the corner, talking to her mum and Emma's.

So, it's been going on for *ages*, she thought angrily, and she hasn't said a *single* word to *me* about him.

She had always thought that she could trust her mother, but now it seemed that she had been wrong. At that moment Tina and Sassy, bored because no one was stroking them any more, came to find Lou and see if there was any milk going. They pushed against the living-room door, which squeaked, and the man looked up. He seemed surprised at the sight of Lou and, seeing his expression, her mother turned around.

'Oh, hello, Lou,' she said. 'How are you feeling? Come and meet Professor Templar.'

Chapter Six

Lou was taken aback. Professor Templar was the man her mum worked for and, of course, she *had* told Lou about him. But Lou had imagined that a professor would be old and bald, with little glasses and a beard. This man wasn't bald or bearded, and he wasn't much older than her mother. He smiled at Lou and said, 'Hello!'

'Hello,' muttered Lou, not very graciously. She glanced at the mugs. '*I* wanted a drink,' she told Jenny accusingly. Why hadn't her mum asked her if she would like some coffee? Because she forgot me, that's why, she thought crossly.

'You looked as if you were asleep,' said her mother mildly.

'Well, I wasn't,' said Lou. 'I was just listening to the tape.' She knew that she sounded sulky but she didn't seem to be able to help the way her voice came out.

Professor Templar got up and looked at his watch. 'Mustn't keep you from your work, Jenny,' he said. 'Thanks for the coffee and do think about what I said.'

Lou's mum smiled and said, 'Yes, I will.'

Lou stared after him as he went. She felt that she had somehow made him go … and she was glad.

When Jenny came back, she looked at Lou thoughtfully and said, 'Is something worrying you?'

Lou wanted to burst into tears and say, 'Yes, I'm afraid you're going to get married again and that my life will go pear-shaped.' But if she did, her mum might say, 'Well, I was waiting for a chance to tell you, Lou ...' and once she had said it, it would all be true and there would be no way Lou could change it. So instead she said, 'Oh, well, it's the audition. I was really awful and they won't know I was ill ...'

Her mother smiled. 'I phoned them after we got back. I told them about the chickenpox.'

'And will they let me do it again?' asked Lou. She didn't want to, not without Jem, but at least it would give her a chance to show them that she didn't usually dance as if she had boots on.

'Well, no,' said Jenny, 'but I'm sure they'll take you.'

Lou looked downcast. They probably thought she was so hopeless that it wasn't worth giving her another chance. She sighed and wandered back to her room. It seemed as if her life was determined to go pear-shaped one way or the other.

By the next day the first spots were beginning to fade … which would have made Lou feel much better, except that new spots were still coming. What made it so unfair was that Jem said he still had only six spots while she was *covered* in them.

'And Jem says all his spots, except one, are where they don't show,' Lou moaned to her mother, 'while most of mine are on my face. I'm just glad he can't see me.'

'Don't you want him to see you?' asked Jenny.

'No, I *don't*,' said Lou very decidedly. 'He'll only tease me.'

'That's a pity,' said Jenny, 'because his gran thought she might bring him over tomorrow. She says he's as bored as you are and it won't hurt him if he comes in the car.'

'Oh, great!' said Lou. 'What time will they be here?'

Her mother grinned. 'You've changed your tune.'

'Oh, yes ... Well, I'd rather be teased than bored.'

'What are you doing today?'

'Don't know. Listen to a tape maybe?'

'Well,' said her mother, 'do you remember that talk we had after you came back from staying with Shell? About whether Jem would do ballet or musicals?'

Lou hadn't forgotten. She wanted Jem to be her partner when she became a famous ballerina. But he said he didn't want to be a ballet dancer, he wanted to do musicals like Shell. When Lou tried to persuade him, he said he didn't want to spend his time standing around, holding her up while she did her arabesques. He wanted something more exciting.

'I thought we might get some ballet videos for you to watch,' said Jenny.

'Only we could look for some with really good parts for men ... like *The Corsair*.'

'Oh, yes!' said Lou. She had seen Rudolph Nureyev doing fantastic leaps in that one. 'But how can we get them by tomorrow?'

'I thought we could search the Internet,' said Jenny, 'to find what's available.'

'Brilliant!' said Lou.

Her mother showed her what to do and Lou found *The Corsair*, danced by the Russian Kirov Ballet, and another ballet called *Spartacus* by the famous Bolshoi Company.

'Now phone the library,' said Jenny, 'and see if they can get either of them.'

Lou was always borrowing books from the library, so the lady who answered knew her quite well. She looked up the ballets on her computer and said they had

Spartacus in stock and they could get *The Corsair* from another branch.

'Tell her I'll call in tomorrow morning,' said Jenny.

'Easy, peasy!' said Lou as she put down the phone.

'The wonders of modern technology,' said Jenny. 'Now let's get some lunch.'

Chapter Seven

Lou was ready with *Spartacus* in the video as she waited for Jem to arrive next day. Her mum had picked it up from the library on her way back from Charlie's playschool.

Lou didn't know anything about Spartacus. She read out the video blurb to her mother and found that he was a slave who had led an uprising against the Romans.

'A lot of fight scenes then,' said Jenny. 'Jem will like that.'

Lou made a face.

'You'd better not look bored if you're watching with Jem,' warned her mother. 'You're trying to prove that ballet is exciting, remember?'

'I suppose so,' said Lou, 'only there won't be much dancing for ballerinas if it's all war stuff.'

'You don't know until you've seen it,' said her mother reasonably.

Unfortunately, when Jem did come, he had brought a new computer game with him. He had been playing it alone all the day before and now he was looking for someone he could thrash. Lou sighed. She knew it was no use trying to change his mind about ballet when he wanted to zap aliens. They played for the next hour but her heart wasn't in it. Jem beat her easily.

'You'll do better next time, now you've got the hang of it,' he said encouragingly.

'Do we have to play it *again*?' said Lou. 'My mum got us a really good ballet video.'

'Just once more. We can watch your video after lunch.'

Lou threw herself into the second game with a fierce concentration. She thought if

she could beat him, he wouldn't want to play it a third time. She found, when she tried, that she was pretty good at it. As the game neared its end, she was slightly ahead.

'We'll make it the best of three,' said Jem, seeing that he was losing.

Oh, no! thought Lou, and at once became all thumbs.

Jem stormed past and beat her by a few points. 'You're getting quite good though,' he told her, sounding unbearably smug.

It was not until after lunch that Lou finally got him to watch *Spartacus*. But from the very opening scene, she knew that he was hooked. For one thing, he couldn't get over the sheer number of male dancers on the stage. There wasn't a ballerina in sight, but there were at least forty men who made up the Roman army. They had been fighting a war and when the chained captives were brought in, there were about twenty more men and all of them were great dancers. Luckily the captives had their womenfolk with them, because by then Lou had got tired of watching soldiers.

Spartacus was the tallest and the handsomest of the captives. His wife, Phrygia, was very beautiful and he tried to protect her when the slave-drivers came with whips to take the women away. In the end they got separated and he was forced to become a gladiator. The Romans made him fight blindfolded against another gladiator and when he won he found that he had killed his brother.

In the second act Spartacus led a revolt

against the Romans and beat them. He
got Phrygia back and they danced a
wonderful *pas de deux* together. Phrygia
had loose dark hair and she didn't wear a

beautiful tutu, just a plain brown tunic. But Lou knew at once that it was a role she had to dance one day.

She sneaked a look at Jem to see what he thought of it. He had gone very quiet, and she saw that his eyes were glued to the screen. Jenny put her head round the door at that moment to see if they wanted a drink, but Jem didn't even notice her. Catching Lou's eye, she raised her eyebrows and smiled. Lou grinned at her and gave her a thumbs-up sign behind Jem's back.

Emma had ballet class after school and by the time she got back Jem had gone home.

'Oh, I wish I could have seen it with you,' she said when Lou told her about *Spartacus*.

'We could watch it now,' suggested

Lou, who couldn't wait to see it again.

'I've got to have my tea and do my homework,' said Emma miserably.

'You could eat with us while we're watching,' offered Lou.

So they munched away in front of the television while Lou zipped through the fighting bits and showed Emma the marvellous *pas de deux*.

'I didn't know there were so many men who did ballet in the *whole world*,' said Emma wonderingly.

'And they're so tall,' said Lou. 'Even when Phrygia is on her points, Spartacus is still taller.'

'And he lifts her up as if she was a little child.'

They watched in silence for a while.

Then Lou said, 'Do you think Jem will be as tall as that?'

'His grandad is pretty tall,' said Emma.

There was another silence while Lou tried to imagine Jem lifting her effortlessly on one arm.

Emma said, 'You look a bit like Phrygia, Lou.'

Lou gave a hollow laugh. 'Not now, I don't.'

Emma glanced at her friend's awful, spotty face. 'Well, no ... But that won't last,' she said. 'I meant when you're grown up.'

Lou watched Phrygia, pale and beautiful, being adored by the handsome Spartacus. 'If only,' she said.

Chapter Eight

Jem came again the next day and this time he didn't bother to bring the video game. The library had got the Kirov video of *The Corsair* from the other branch, so they watched that first. It had some good parts for male dancers, with a lot of leaping about, but neither of them liked it as much as *Spartacus*. So they put on the Bolshoi tape again and Lou was pleased when Jem fast-forwarded through some of the fighting scenes to get to Spartacus's solo dances. Lou wanted to see Phrygia's solos too and they both wanted to watch the *pas de deux* again. Lou felt certain that Jem was imagining himself as Spartacus, just as she wanted to dance Phrygia's role. Jem couldn't say about this ballet that it was all 'prancing about in embroidered jackets'.

They watched it through to the end. Spartacus was betrayed and the Romans killed him. At the moment of his death he was raised high into the air, with all the lances of the Roman soldiers pointing up at him. It looked very dramatic and Jem said, 'Now *that's* a ballet part it would be worth dancing!'

'Worth all the lessons and the practice?' asked Lou.

Jem glanced at her and grinned. 'Yes, I guess so,' he said.

Lou wanted to say, 'So will you give up musicals and do ballet then?' but she remembered her mother's warning: 'You can't *make* Jem do ballet, Lou. *He* has to *want* to do it. He'll make his own decision when he's older.' But that doesn't mean I can't give him a good shove in the right direction, thought Lou.

'Could I take the tape home tonight?' Jem asked. 'I'd like my gran and grandad to see it.'

Yes! thought Lou triumphantly, but she hesitated. 'I said Mrs Dillon could borrow it tonight,' she explained. 'She wants to see it because it's the Bolshoi.'

Jem looked disappointed.

'You can take it when you come tomorrow,' said Lou.

But Jem said, 'I'm going back to school tomorrow.'

Lou stared at him. 'What about the chickenpox?' she protested. 'I mean, you got it after me!'

'Yes, but I haven't had any new spots

for days, and the six spots I have got are where they don't show.'

'Except for that one on the end of your nose,' said Lou cruelly.

Jem crossed his eyes trying to see it. 'I can live with that one,' he said.

Lou was really fed up. She had found a few new spots only the day before, so she would be stuck at home alone for ages.

'It's not fair,' she moaned, 'and I'm missing all my ballet lessons. I was ill for the audition and now I'll be hopelessly out of practice for the grade exam. It's only a couple of weeks away!'

'Ten days,' said Jem.

'Even worse! And if I can't practise, horrible old Angela will beat me!'

'Can't you practise with Mrs Dillon?' suggested Jem.

'I thought of that,' said Lou, 'but Mum

says old people are supposed to stay away from children with chickenpox.'

Lou told Jenny about Jem wanting to borrow the tape and when it was time for him to go home, she said, 'I've had a word with Mrs Dillon, Jem. She's quite happy to wait for a couple of days and we've got the tape for a week.'

So Jem took *Spartacus* home with him. Lou and her mother stood at the window and watched them go. They could hear Jem telling his grandmother what a great ballet it was as they got into the car.

'Nice one, Lou,' said her mother.

'Well, it was your idea,' said Lou.

They looked at one another and smiled.

Emma came down after school with some good news.

'My dad got that job in Cornwall,' she

told Lou. 'The one with your gran's friend.'

'Oh, great!' said Lou.

'Yes, and he says he'll be working down there through most of the summer holidays and maybe mum and Martin and me can go too.'

Lou wasn't so sure about that. 'What, *all* the holidays?'

'Yes, I think so. Won't you be staying down there with your granny and grandad?'

'Well, we usually go for a few weeks,' said Lou, 'but not for the whole time. You'd be away for ages and I'm fed up with being on my own.'

Emma thought about it. 'You could come and stay with us,' she said. 'When you're not at your gran's, I mean. I'll go and ask my mum.' She started off upstairs

but then paused half-way. She turned and came slowly down again. 'There was something else, Lou,' she said. 'I forgot it when my dad told me about Cornwall.'

'What is it?' asked Lou, alarmed by her friend's worried face.

'Well,' said Emma, 'I heard my dad say to my mum, "Lou does need a bigger room. It will be much better for her." They stopped talking about you when I went into the room, and then Dad told me about Cornwall instead. Oh, Lou, do you think your mum really *is* going to move away?'

Chapter Nine

Lou couldn't bring herself to ask her mother what was going on, but she needed to talk to someone about it. So she swore Emma to secrecy and told her all her worries about Professor Templar.

'What is he like?' asked Emma, wide-eyed.

'Well, all right, I suppose,' said Lou. 'But that's not the point. I don't want a stepfather. You know how Paul and his

stepfather were always quarrelling.'

'I don't think it's so bad now,' said
Emma. 'In fact, I think Paul quite likes
him.'

But Lou wasn't looking for comfort; she
wanted support in the war against
stepfathers.

'We'd have to move away,' she pointed

out. 'I expect he'd make us go and live in his house. I mean, there's no room for another person in this flat.'

Emma certainly didn't want to lose Lou.

'Do you think that's what my dad meant about you having a bigger room?'

'Well, it all fits, doesn't it?' said Lou.

'Ask your mum about him,' said Emma. 'It would be better to know.'

But Lou shook her head. There was no way she was going to give her mum a chance to tell her the bad news.

The next day was very boring with Emma and Jem both at school. It hadn't been so bad being at home when she was ill, but now she felt fine and it was miserable without her friends. Even Charlie was at playschool, and her mother was busy working.

'One more day without any new spots,' said Jenny, 'and they will let you go back to school.'

They searched Lou all over and found no new blisters, only lots of brown scabs, and some of those were falling off.

Professor Templar came again in the afternoon to pick up some work her mother had finished. Lou saw his car outside and found that she urgently needed a drink, so she tiptoed through to the kitchen, pausing outside the living-room door. A moment later she wished that she hadn't, because she heard her mum say, 'It's a big decision, Michael. I have to think how it will affect the children,' and Professor Templar said, 'It might be difficult for a while, but in the long term it must mean a better life for you all.'

Lou turned and went silently back to her room. She found that she didn't need the drink after all. It's true, she thought. She *is* going to get married again … and she felt like crying.

Lou was glad to be back at school, even though she kept worrying about what her mother might be up to while she was away.

Mercifully, her red spots had faded and, if the boys teased her a bit about the scabs, the girls were mostly kind.

'Oh, *poor* Lou,' cried Tracey. 'It must be so *awful* to be all *scabby* like that!'

'Thanks a lot, Trace,' said Lou, feeling that she could have done without *that* bit of sympathy.

*

The next evening they had ballet class. The grade exam was less than a week away and Lou was really out of practice. Her scabby arms and legs no longer seemed to know the precise feel of each position. She had to keep her mind focused on every small movement to get it right. She was afraid Mrs Dennison might say she wasn't ready for the next grade, but her teacher just smiled and said, 'Well done, Lucy, you worked very hard today.'

As she walked home from the Maple School with Emma and Jem, Lou thought how good it was to have her life back in its old pattern.

Jem gave back the *Spartacus* tape so that Lou could lend it to Mrs Dillon. He said that his gran and grandad had really enjoyed it and had promised to take him to see the Bolshoi next time they came to London.

'We could all go together,' said Lou, 'and Mrs Dillon too. It would make a brilliant outing.'

Then Emma asked the question Lou hadn't dared to ask. 'Do you think you might do ballet after all, Jem?'

He glanced sideways at her and smiled. 'If I could dance Spartacus, Em, I think I might.' And then he added, 'But I haven't made up my mind yet, so *don't* go around telling everyone.'

'I *never* tell secrets,' said Lou proudly, and Emma promised him that she wouldn't either.

By the day of the grade exam, the scabs had all gone. This gave Lou a bit of comfort, but not a lot, because she knew

that she still wasn't back to her usual
form. Suppose the Junior Associates
assessors were waiting to see how she did

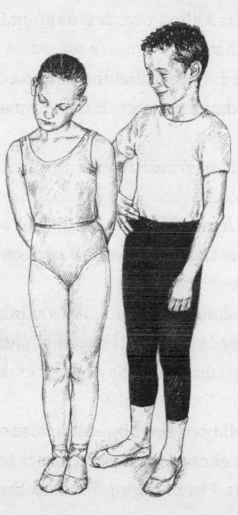

in the grade exam? A bad audition *and* a poor grade might put an end to all her hopes.

As she waited her turn to go in, she found that she wasn't as scared as she had been the year before, because she knew what to expect. But she wasn't happy.

'Cheer up!' said Jenny. 'I'm sure you'll be fine.'

And Jem said, 'You know you're always brilliant, Lou, once you're in front of an audience.'

Lou shook her head. 'An examiner isn't the same,' she said. 'I mean, an audience *wants* to like you. They're not looking out for every little mistake.'

She did her best, but afterwards, eating cream cakes in the Cosy Corner tea-room and listening to Jem and Emma happily swapping notes, she couldn't shake off a sense of disappointment. The exam just came too soon, she thought. If I'd had another week to practise, I would have been OK.

Chapter Ten

Emma had asked her mum if Lou could stay with them in Cornwall. Mrs Browne said that she would be very happy to take her with them … only it wasn't that simple. She had been trying to find a cottage to rent but they all seemed to be booked up during the school holidays.

'It may not be possible for us to go at all,' she told the girls. 'And if we do find somewhere, it might not have room to take Lou too.'

Emma was really disappointed, but when they were alone in Emma's room, Lou said, 'Actually, Em, I'm not sure I'd *want* to be away from my mum for too long.'

Emma understood at once. 'Because of Professor Templar?' she said.

Lou nodded. 'I might come back and find it was all settled,' she said gloomily.

But the next day there was good news.

'Grandma phoned,' said her mother when Lou came in from school. 'She and grandad want to go to Canada for a while to be with Auntie Helen when the baby is born. She has asked us to look after the house all through the school holidays and take care of the dog and cat.'

'Oh, fantastic!' said Lou. 'So Emma can come and stay with us?'

'Of course,' said Jenny, 'and her mum and dad too. It's a big house.'

Lou raced upstairs to tell Emma. They hugged each other with excitement.

'And the best thing,' said Lou, 'is that my mum will be a long way away from *him* all summer.'

Emma didn't need to ask who *he* was.

When the grade exam results went up at the Maple School, Lou couldn't bear to look at the list. She had been the same the year before, but then she had done better than her wildest hopes.

This time she knew from Jem's wary look as he came back from the board that the news was not so good.

'Did you get your Distinction?' she asked him.

'Yes,' he told her without excitement.

'Oh, great! And Emma?' she added quickly.

'Commended.'

'She'll be thrilled.'

'You were Highly Commended, Lou, which is pretty brilliant considering ...'

Lou swallowed. 'Thanks,' she said. She had had a Distinction the year before. 'And Angela?' she asked.

'Highly Commended,' he told her.

It was a small crumb of comfort. If Angela had got a Distinction she would have queened it over Lou for a whole year. She put a big smile on her face and went to congratulate Emma.

Lou tried hard not to think about the Junior Associates. She knew that the results took a long time to come, because the auditions went on for weeks. When she did think about it, it was always the same. She felt sure that Jem would get a place and Angela too, but that she would be left out. And then her ballet lessons at the Maple School would never be the same again … not with Angela in the changing room every week, telling everyone in her loud, posh voice how *marvellous* it was to be having classes at the *Royal Ballet School*.

And then one day Lou's mum was waiting when she got home from school. Emma had gone to her piano lesson, so Lou came in through the basement door. As she closed it behind her, Jenny came out of the kitchen and handed her a letter. It was addressed to Mrs Lambert and it had already been opened.

Lou turned pale but her mother said, 'Take it out and read it.'

Lou opened the letter and felt her heart race. She read, 'Dear Mrs Lambert, We are pleased to be able to offer your daughter Lucy a place ...'

It was all too much and Lou burst into a flood of tears.

Jenny hugged her and said, 'You're not supposed to cry, silly. You're supposed to be happy.'

'I *am* happy,' sniffed Lou. 'What about Jem?'

'His gran phoned,' said her mum. 'He got a place too.'

Jenny made two mugs of chocolate and they sat at the kitchen table reading the letter over and over again.

'So, will you be a bit happier now?' asked her mother. 'I know how worried you've been the last few weeks.'

Lou sighed before she could help it and then tried to smile. It didn't fool her mum.

'Come on,' she said. 'There's something else, isn't there? Do you want to tell me what it is?'

Lou thought she could risk telling part of it.

'It was something Emma heard ... Mr Browne said I was going to have a bigger room. I thought we must be going to move ... and that *you* weren't telling me.'

'Oh dear,' said her mother. 'Is that all?' She thought for a moment and then said, 'Well, it's true, you are going to have a bigger room, but we're *not* moving.'

'Then how?'

'While we are away in Cornwall, the

builders are coming in to build an extension to the basement … at the back, where the garden is lower. It will mean a lot of extra space for us. Charlie will take over your little bedroom and you will have a new one with a window on to the garden.'

Lou couldn't believe her luck. 'But why didn't you *tell* me?' she said.

'Well,' said her mother, 'it was all Mr Browne's idea and he wanted it to be a surprise.'

Lou was thinking fast. If they weren't going to move, then her mum couldn't be getting married again … unless the extra space was because …

'Come on, Lou,' said Jenny. 'I know you too well. What else is bothering you?'

So in the end Lou told her what she had heard Professor Templar say.

Her mother looked puzzled. 'And what did you think we were talking about?' she asked.

Lou gulped. 'I thought … I thought you were going to get married again,' she muttered.

Her mother stared at her for a long moment and Lou couldn't tell if she was cross or what. 'I thought my life would go all pear-shaped,' she said indignantly.

Then Jenny began to laugh, and she went on laughing. 'Oh, Lou,' she said at last. 'When *will* you stop listening at keyholes? Professor Templar thinks I should go back to college, to finish my degree course. I was half-way through it when Daddy and I got married and I found I was expecting you. And if I do go back, we'll be a bit short of money again, which is why we can't afford to move and why Mr Browne is making the flat bigger for us.'

Suddenly it all made sense and Lou could see that she had been really silly.

'Next time you are worried about something,' said her mum, 'come and talk to me. Promise, Lou?'

'I promise!' said Lou, hugging her again. It seemed that everything would be all right after all.

She heard the top door open. 'That'll be Emma,' she said. 'I'd better go up and tell her the good news!'

Dancing Shoes

Hi!

Isn't it brilliant? Jem and I both get to go to the Junior Associates class. I was so worried that everything would go pear-shaped.

I can't wait for the summer holidays in Cornwall — especially now, because everyone is coming to stay: Emma, Jem, Shell and Mrs Dillon. It's going to be such a laugh, and you never know, we might get to do some ballet . . .

Love

Lou

PS Find out what happens in *Dancing Shoes: Dance to the Rescue.* Don't miss it!